# HORRIBLE HARRY
## AT
# HALLOWEEN

# HORRIBLE HARRY
## AT
# HALLOWEEN

BY SUZY KLINE

pictures by Frank Remkiewicz

VIKING

VIKING
Published by the Penguin Group,
Penguin Putnam Books for Young Readers,
345 Hudson Street, New York, New York 10014, U.S.A.
Penguin Books Ltd, 27 Wrights Lane, London W8 5TZ, England
Penguin Books Australia Ltd, Ringwood, Victoria, Australia
Penguin Books Canada Ltd, 10 Alcorn Avenue,
Toronto, Ontario, Canada M4V 3B2
Penguin Books (N.Z.) Ltd,
182-190 Wairau Road, Auckland 10, New Zealand

Penguin Books Ltd, Registered Offices:
Harmondsworth, Middlesex, England

First published in 2000 by Viking,
a division of Penguin Putnam Books for Young Readers.

10  9  8  7  6  5  4

LIBRARY OF CONGRESS CATALOGING-IN-PUBLICATION DATA
Kline, Suzy.
Horrible Harry at Halloween/by Suzy Kline ;
illustrated by Frank Remkiewicz.
    p. cm.
Summary: The students in Miss Mackle's third-grade class enjoy a day
of Halloween surprises, including Harry's unusual costume.
ISBN 0-670-88864-8
[1. Schools—Fiction. 2. Halloween—Fiction.] I. Remkiewicz, Frank, ill. II.
Title. PZ7.K6797 Hnt 2000 [Fic]—dc21 00-028995

Printed in U.S.A.
Set in New Century Schoolbook

Special appreciation to . . .
my editor, Cathy Hennessy, for her helpful insight,
my husband, Rufus, for his valuable comments,
and love for old TV shows,
and my former student Heath Jenkins, who
drenched the front row with his water experiment.

# Contents

# What's Harry Going to Be?

Every Halloween we wear costumes to South School. The biggest question the week before is . . .

What's Harry going to be?

My name is Doug. I'm in third grade. My best friend is Harry. He loves horrible things. His name is even spooky, Harry *Spooger*. When it's Halloween, Harry always plays a few tricks on us.

And each year his costumes get scarier and scarier.

The day before Halloween we were sitting on the rug in the library corner. The second morning bell hadn't rung yet, so we were just talking about the big question . . . *What's Harry going to be?*

"Remember last year in second grade?" Sidney said. "Harry wore a snake costume. All you could see was his white teeth. He was *so* scary!"

"He was *late,*" Mary groaned. "It took him ten extra minutes to slither across the playground. I remember he had to stay after school that day."

As Mary thought about it more, she smiled.

"I remember what costume Harry wore in the first grade," Song Lee said. "He was the Loch Ness Monster."

Sidney's teeth began to chatter. "He was all slimy and green."

"Yeah, even in kindergarten Harry was scary," I said. "Remember? He was Count Dracula. He chewed on strawberries and let the red juice drip down his chin like *blood*."

Mary shivered. "Well, I'm going to be Tinker Bell. I found a fancy gold dress with gold sequins at the thrift shop for five dollars. Mom is taking up the hem, and making me a wand and a special box with magic powder in it. It's called pixie dust."

"Oooh! You'll have magical powers!" Song Lee exclaimed.

No one else ooohed.

"Hey, what are you wearing?" I asked Dexter.

"The usual. My Elvis costume. I'm bringing a guitar, too."

"Cool," I said. "What are you gonna be Sid?"

"A squid," a voice said from the doorway.

*"Harry!"* we all replied as he ran into the room and took a flying leap onto the space couch. It was finally his turn to sit on it. We go in ABC order. Spooger is last. It was his day.

"What are you wearing Harry?" Mary asked.

"Ahhhhhhhh," he replied lying back on the couch. His head was propped up on the little cushion.

"Huh?" Mary nagged. "I'm going to be Tinker Bell."

"Well Tink, you'll never guess what

I'm gonna be in a thousand years," Harry said putting his arms behind his head.

"A Komodo dragon?" Song Lee asked.

"Nope."

"T-Rex?" I asked.

"Nope."

"A ghost? A ghoul? A vampire?" Mary persisted.

"Nope. Nope. Nope."

*"Harry!"* we all groaned. *"Tell us!"*

But Harry didn't. He just shook his head and changed the subject. "I thought of a new game we can play for recess today."

"What?" we replied.

"Tombstone kickball. We get some chalk and draw a tombstone on first base, second base, third base, and home plate."

"Neat-o!" Dexter and I said.

Suddenly, Sidney leaped in the air. "Now I know what you're gonna be for Halloween . . . a *walking corpse!* That's why you've got graveyards on the brain."

"Wrong again, Squid. You'll just have to wait until tomorrow." And then Harry closed his eyes and pretended to snore.

# Water, Water Everywhere!

That morning we did science experiments with water. Everybody paid attention except for Sidney. He kept bugging Harry about his Halloween costume.

"Are you going to be a mummy?"

Harry laughed. "Nope."

"Give it up, Sid," Mary scolded. "It's *my* turn now to go up and do an experiment. I don't want you to distract anyone. So . . . *shhhh!*"

We watched Mary take a big brown bag to the front of the room. Two big words were written in cursive on the blackboard:

*Water Experiments*

Miss Mackle had an empty aquarium, plastic containers, and four jugs of water set up on a side table. Mary set her bag down on a desktop.

"These are the materials you need to do my experiment," she explained as she pointed to each one. "A glass, oil, food coloring, and a spoon. Now I will tell you about each step.

"First, you fill the glass with water. I'm adding orange coloring for Halloween.

"Then you drop a spoonful of oil in the glass.

"See what happens?"

"I can't see," Sidney complained.

"Me either," Ida said.

Mary held the glass up in the air. "The oil and water do not mix. The oil is just floating around the top like beads."

"Cool," Dexter said.

"I knew that already," Harry said.

Mary shot Harry a look.

"Wonderful job, Mary!" Miss Mackle exclaimed as she recorded a grade in her red book.

Suddenly, Harry sneezed.

Right on the back of Mary's head.

Mary turned around. "Aaaugh!" she complained. "Why don't you use a tissue?"

"Don't need to," Harry said. Then he pulled a white hankie out of his back pocket. "See?"

It had two big boogers on it.

"You're so *gross!*" Mary groaned.

When she turned around, Harry showed me the boogers up close. They were just raisins.

"It's an old joke," he whispered. "But Mary fell for it."

Harry and his Halloween tricks! They were just beginning. . . .

"Harry Spooger?" Miss Mackle called. "You're next."

Mary folded her arms.

Harry took his backpack with him to the front of the room. Carefully he put the aquarium tank on Mary's desk and started filling it with water.

After we watched him empty three jugs into the tank, Harry opened up his backpack.

"See if you can guess which things will sink or float," he said.

First he pulled out a pumpkin. "Who thinks this will sink?"

Everybody raised their hands.

Harry dropped the pumpkin into the water. It made a big splash, dipped under the water, and then popped back up!

*"It floats!"* everyone shouted.

"Tricked ya!" Harry grinned. Next, he held up a potato. Harry had drawn a face on it with a black marker. It looked like a shrunken head. "Do you think this will sink or float?"

*"Float!"* everyone replied.

Harry dropped the potato into the tank.

It sank to the bottom.

"Tricked ya again!" Harry snorted.

Mary started to pout. "I'll get the next one!" she said. "For sure!"

Harry cackled as he held up one purple grape. I noticed there was a black

dot colored in the middle. It looked like
an eyeball. "Sink or float?"

This time no one called out anything.
People were still thinking.

"Float," Mary said first.

*"Float!"* some other people agreed.

"Sink," said Song Lee.

Harry dropped the purple grape into the tank. It sank to the bottom next to the potato.

Mary made a face.

Harry explained everything like he was a professor. "If something has air pockets, like a pumpkin or lemon, it floats. If it's solid, like a potato or grape, it sinks. I tricked ya today in science. I'll trick ya some more on Halloween!"

Most people groaned, but Song Lee and I smiled. Miss Mackle clapped. "Great job, Harry."

Song Lee went last. She filled a plastic jack-o'-lantern with water. It had a short rope tied to the handle. "I will show you how centrifugal force works."

First she stepped as far as she could away from the blackboard. "Will the people in the front row please put their heads down?"

They did, but their eyes looked up.

Then Song Lee twirled the bucket over her head. We gasped as she swung it around and around.

Miss Mackle's eyes almost popped out of their sockets. The water stayed in the bucket! Not one drop fell out.

When Song Lee stopped, everyone shouted, *"Do it again!"*

"Please do! I'll get my camera this time," Miss Mackle said running to her desk.

Song Lee began her experiment again. But this time, just as she brought the bucket up, she accidentally hit the corner of Mary's desk, and waves of water splashed everywhere!

Everyone laughed but Mary.

She got drenched.

"Hey Mare," Harry snickered. "You should be a sprite for Halloween. That's a water fairy."

Mary blew her wet bangs in the air. "Harry Spooger, one of these days I'm going to get you back!"

# Halloween Day

The next morning, I galloped into the classroom. I was the first one there on Halloween! Dad had to drop me off ten minutes early. He had some kind of meeting.

Miss Mackle was dressed as a witch. She was at the science table cutting the tops off two pumpkins. A very big pumpkin sat on one cookie tray, and a small one sat on another.

I whinnied like a horse. *"Nnneeyehaa!"*

Miss Mackle jumped. *"Oh!* You scared me, Doug!" she said. "I love your centaur costume! Half man and half horse!"

"Thanks," I said. "I've been reading a book about myths from the library."

The teacher beamed. "Wonderful! I think you'll like the story I'm reading this morning. There's a horse in it and it's spooky."

"Cool," I said. Then I galloped over to the pumpkin table.

"Can I help scoop out the seeds?"

"You sure can, Doug. I'd appreciate your help. It's slimy stuff! I listed the seed estimates we made yesterday on this chart. We'll see how it turns out

today when the class actually counts the seeds."

"Yeah," I said. "Everyone thinks there's lots more seeds in the big pumpkin than in the little pumpkin."

Ten minutes later, I had all the seeds out on the trays ready for counting. Just as I was washing the orange slime from my hands, the first bell rang. I quickly dried my hands and raced over to the doorway and waited for the kids.

Mary danced into the room waving a silver wand. Tiny bells were sewed on her hem so she tinkled as she moved. "Make a wish!" she exclaimed.

Miss Mackle closed her eyes. "I wish . . . that everyone would get 100 percent on their spelling test."

Mary opened her gold satin box and sprinkled some pixie dust on her wand.

Then she touched Miss Mackle's head three times with the wand. "Your wish is granted!"

Just as the teacher clapped her green hands, Ida leaped into the room. *"Meow!"* she said as she clawed the air.

She was wearing a black cat costume.

Song Lee came in wearing blue pants and a blue shirt. Her hair was completely tucked inside a white cap. She wore latex gloves and a stethoscope around her neck. She went over to Mary and listened to her chest. "Good heartbeat," she said.

"Thank you Dr. Park," Mary replied. "Did you scrub your hands for surgery?"

"Of course," Song Lee answered.

When we heard someone singing, "You ain't nothin' but a hound dog," in the hallway, we knew who was coming next.

Dexter dressed like Elvis.

"So where's Harry?" Mary asked. I could tell she was curious about his costume.

We all looked around.

"He hasn't showed up yet," I said.

"Someone's coming now," Mary said pointing to the door with her wand.

It was a big brown Kodiak bear.

"Harry?" we all called.

The mystery person took off his bear head.

"It's me . . . *Sidney!*"

"You're one hairy dude," Dexter said.

"Cool, huh? Mom made it from a fake fur coat." Then he growled in Mary's face. *"Grrrrr!"*

"Don't growl at me!" Mary snapped. "I might change you into a frog with my magic wand! It just needs a little more pixie dust."

Everyone watched Mary take a pinch of pixie dust out of her gold satin box and sprinkle it over her wand.

Sidney made a face. "That stuff looks like baby powder. My aunt uses it on my little cousin. It keeps his bottom dry."

"It's *magic pixie dust* for Halloween," Mary insisted.

Sidney sniffed the air. "It smells just like baby powder." Then he put his bear head back on. "Where's Harry?" he asked in a muffled voice.

"The second bell is about to ring," Miss Mackle said. "It's time to return to your seats, boys and girls. You'll find a Halloween search-a-word on your desk."

Mary was the first to sit down. "I bet we won't be able to tell Harry's disguise," she said. "But the next person in the room has *got* to be Harry. He's the only one not here."

The red second hand kept hopping closer to the twelve. Everyone moved their eyes from the wall clock to the doorway, then from the doorway back to the clock.

No one started their Halloween
search-a-word. No one wanted to miss
what Harry was going to be this year!

Suddenly, Mary got an idea. She
popped out of her seat, tinkled her
bells, and waved her wand. A puffy
white cloud filled the air. "Magic pixie

dust, make Harry appear at the door!"

Three seconds later, the bell rang, and Harry walked in.

# Harry Arrives!

We must have stared at Harry for ten seconds. No one said a word.

Finally, Mary broke the silence. "That's no costume. Who are you supposed to be?"

We all looked at Harry's neatly combed hair, and his suit and tie. His shoes were even polished.

Sidney took off his bear head and

placed it on his desk. I think it was
making him hot. His forehead was
dripping wet. "You just get out of
church, Harry?" he asked.

Harry slowly reached in his jacket,
and pulled something out. It was a silver badge with the number 714 on it.
When he talked, he used a business
tone. He was very matter-of-fact.

"My name is Sergeant Joe Friday. I
carry a badge. I'm from the Los

Angeles Police Department. When there's a crime, *that's* when I go to work."

Mary started to make fun of Harry. "You're not scary or even horrible this year. You're just acting silly!"

Harry shot Mary a look. "Silly? Joe Friday is smart. He solves crimes."

Mary scoffed. *"Puleeze!"*

Miss Mackle walked over to Harry. "Hello, Sergeant Friday. I know who you are. I used to watch *Dragnet* all the time when I was growing up. How do you know about him?"

Harry answered like a detective. "I watch old-time TV, ma'am. Tuesday and Thursday, six-thirty P.M., WNBX, Channel Thirty-three."

"Well, Sergeant Friday," Miss

Mackle said. "You certainly know your facts."

"Yes ma'am, just the facts. And this is where I keep 'em." Then Harry took a notebook out of his pocket and held it up.

Mary and some of the other kids giggled.

That morning, shortly after the pledge, Miss Mackle turned off the lights. "I'm going to read you one of my favorite Halloween stories, "The Headless Horseman," adapted from Washington Irving's classic *The Legend of Sleepy Hollow*."

Then she handed two students flashlights and sat down on the teacher's chair in front of the room. "Shine the light on me as I read, please."

As soon as Ida and Dexter did, Miss Mackle's witch face lit up like a jack-o'-lantern. The raisins that were on her chin and nose really looked like warts. There was a large shadow of her head and hat just behind her on the blackboard.

"Ooooooh," we responded.

We all leaned forward as Miss Mackle read the story about Ichabod Crane and his spooky ride through Sleepy Hollow.

You could hear a pin drop.

When she finished the story, someone started making a horrible groaning sound . . . "Ooooooooh! Ooooooooh!" It sounded like they had a bad stomachache. "Ooooooooh! Ooooooooh!"

As soon as Miss Mackle turned on

the lights, we discovered who it was.

"It's Sergeant Joe Friday! Look at him!" Mary yelled.

Everyone turned and stared at Harry. His suit was up over his head. He looked like he was headless.

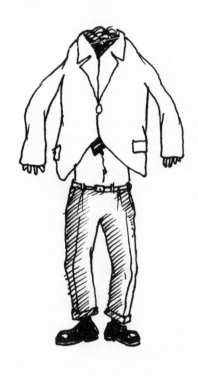

Miss Mackle laughed.

We laughed, too.

Suddenly, the teacher stepped outside the classroom. When she returned, she whispered, "Boys and girls, the music teacher is just coming down the hall. Let's have some fun like Harry." Then she pulled her witch cape over her head.

Quickly everyone moved their costumes up over their heads, and waited quietly for Mr. Marks to enter the classroom.

We could hear his footsteps as he got closer. He was humming as usual. "La ti da ti dah . . ."

As he entered our room, we heard him scream, *"Aaaaauuuuugh! A class with no heads!"*

"*Happy Halloween!*" we shouted, before we popped our heads out.

"Ahhhh," Mr. Marks sighed. "What a surprise!" he said. "You sure fooled me."

We clapped and cheered. We had no idea that the *next* surprise was going to be on us.

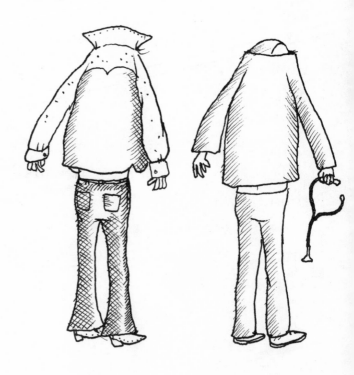

# "The Case of the Missing Pixie Dust"

It happened that afternoon during math. Sergeant Joe Friday was collecting facts in his notebook. When we finished counting the pumpkin seeds, Harry wrote 583 for the small pumpkin, and 588 seeds for the bigger one.

"Hmmm," Harry said, "the only real difference was that the bigger pumpkin had bigger seeds."

"Yeah," I agreed. "You're right, Joe."

After Ida and Dexter took the trays of pumpkin seeds to the kitchen, Miss Mackle began drawing a Halloween bar graph on the chalkboard.

"So, what categories could we have for the costumes we're wearing today?"

"Well," Mary said. "There's a king and a jester in our class, and I'm Tinker Bell, so we could be fairy-tale costumes."

Harry scribbled three tally marks for the fairy-tale category in his notebook and then put the pencil stub he was using on his ear.

"Good idea!" Miss Mackle said. "Maybe we could make it fairy tales/myths and include the centaur."

I whinnied. *"Nnneeyehaa."*

Harry added another tally mark.

"Other categories?" the teacher asked.

"Animal costumes," Sidney answered. Then he growled, *"Grrrrrr!"*

*"Meow!"* Ida said as she clawed the air.

"Scary costumes," someone said.

"Great!" Miss Mackle replied, writing the titles down on the board. "But what about a category for our surgeon, singer, detective, and astronaut?"

Song Lee, Dexter, Harry, and Miguel smiled. Those were their costumes.

"Jobs?" Song Lee suggested.

"Yes!" Miss Mackle replied. "Sometimes we call them occupations."

Suddenly, Mary screamed, *"Someone stole my pixie dust! There's a thief in the room!"*

Everyone jumped off their chair a few inches. What a surprise!

Harry leaped out of his seat. He was at Mary's desk in a flash. His notebook was already open. He just snatched his pencil stub off his ear. "The facts, ma'am, just the facts."

"Oh Harry!" Mary said as she held up her box. "I'm not playing any games. This is for *real*. My pixie dust is gone! See!"

Everyone stared at Mary's empty gold satin box.

"I have a job to do," Harry replied. "I carry a badge. I'm Sergeant Joe Friday from the—"

"Los Angeles Police Department," Mary snapped.

Harry looked at his watch, then wrote down the time. "It's two-oh-two P.M. When do you last remember seeing the dust in the box?"

Mary thought about it. "When I took it down to lunch. It was part of my costume."

"Did you have hot or cold lunch, ma'am?"

"Hot."

Harry walked over to the lunch menu that was taped on the wall. He reviewed the facts. "Friday, October thirty-first, cheese pizza, tossed salad, carrot sticks, pumpkin cookies . . ."

We watched Harry jot it down. When he returned to Mary's desk, he fired one question after another. "Where did you keep the box when you were eating lunch?"

"On my tray."

"All the time, ma'am?"

"Well," Mary paused, "when I had to stack my tray, I put it on the counter."

"For how long, ma'am?"

Mary bit her lip. "A minute? Mrs. Thunderburke said I made a beautiful Tinker Bell. I was showing her the tiny bells on my hem."

"I see, ma'am."

*"Do you have to say ma'am?"* Mary yelled.

"Yes ma'am," Harry replied.

It was hard not to laugh, but we quieted down quickly. We didn't want to miss any facts about the crime.

"Who was behind you in line, ma'am?"

Mary pointed at the bear. "Sidney!"

Harry walked over to Sidney's desk. "Do you know anything about the box?"

Sidney's response was hard to understand.

"Can you speak louder, sir?" Harry asked.

Miss Mackle sat down on a desktop. "Sidney, aren't you hot in that headpiece?" she asked.

While Sidney mumbled something, Harry sniffed Sidney's fur.

"Just as I thought," Harry said.

"What?" Mary replied.

"Baby powder," Harry said. "He smells like baby powder."

"Sidney!" Mary gasped. "*You* did it! You're the thief!"

Harry stared at Sidney's blue eyes through the little round holes of his costume. "Do you want to tell us about it, Sid?"

Maybe it was Harry's businesslike tone. Maybe Sidney was just hot. Sidney did what Harry asked. He confessed.

We all watched Sidney slowly pull off his bear headpiece. Baby powder was smeared over his forehead.

"I . . . just meant to use a little," Sidney confessed. "Mary left it on the counter when she returned her lunch tray. I was so hot. My forehead was dripping. I thought the baby powder might feel cool on my skin. So I took some. I didn't mean to use it *all*. The box just fell out of my hands. When I put it back on the counter, it . . . was empty."

Mary gritted her teeth and growled.

"I'm sorry, Mary!" Sidney said. Then he put his head down on his desk.

Miss Mackle came over. "I think Sidney feels bad about what happened, Mary. But, Sidney, you need to remember to ask first before you use something, and to tell the truth. Maybe you can make it up to Mary."

Mary folded her arms. "Fat chance. The pixie dust was an important part of my Tinker Bell costume for Halloween. I was going to take it with me tonight when I go trick-or-treating."

"Ma'am?" Harry asked. "Can't you put more baby powder in your box for tonight?"

"I guess so," Mary grumbled.

Harry seemed satisfied and returned to his seat. "It's two-thirteen P.M.," he noted. "Case closed."

Miss Mackle looked over at Harry.

"Thank you, Sergeant Friday for being so helpful."

Harry flashed his white teeth as he put his stub pencil back in the cigar box in his desk.

Just then Mrs. Thunderburke showed up in the doorway. "Happy Halloween, boys and girls! Your pumpkin seeds are roasted and ready!"

As everyone cheered, I ran up to Mrs. Thunderburke. "Harry just solved the Case of the Missing Pixie Dust," I said. "Just like a real detective."

"You don't say?" Mrs. Thunderburke replied.

"Just doing my job, ma'am," Harry said taking out his badge. "Sergeant Joe Friday from the Los Angeles Police Department."

Mary rolled her eyeballs.

But Harry *did* do his job. And he made Halloween more fun.

He played his usual tricks on the class, but this year he *really* surprised us with his costume. He wasn't even scary!

And that was the biggest surprise of all!